The Drawing Board

Erikka + Tom,

Thanks for reading my
book. I hope you enjoy!

Love,

Shannon Hofer Pottala

THE DRAWING BOARD

A SHORT STORY COLLECTION

Shannon Hofer-Pottala

Seity House Publishing
Minneapolis, MN

ISBN: 978-0-578-82085-9 (Paperback Edition)

This is a work of fiction. Any references to historical events, real people, or real places are used fictitiously. Names, characters, and places are products of the author's imagination.

Edited by Olivia McGovern.
Front cover image and illustrations by Shannon Hofer-Pottala.
Book design by Shannon Hofer-Pottala.

Printed by Amazon.
First printing edition 2020.

Seity House Publishing
Minneapolis, MN
hoferpottala@gmail.com

Visit www.shannonhp.com

*For my mom, whose love of
words inspired my own*

Contents

A Cup of Cocoa

Isaac watched the flurries of snow outside wrestle one another against the window of the cozy coffee shop. In his opinion, winter was the shop's best season. There was something about the frostiness outside that made the drinks within especially warm; the coffee seemed sharper and the cocoa seemed meltier. He—that is, he and Aisha and Jackson—had visited Drinks by Laila every Tuesday for their entire high school career. All four years and they had not missed a single Tuesday. Then, of course, college hit, and they were lucky to get in four coffee excursions a year, with Aisha in New York for architecture and Isaac staying in Wyoming for business and Jackson—well, Jackson was dead.

A gust of icy winter air bit Isaac's skin and he looked

again toward the shop's door. Aisha stood, her figure temporarily a shadow as Isaac's eyes adjusted to the vicious white of the outside snow. He didn't need to see her face to know her. He recognized her by the sideways puffball on top of her olive green hat, the one that she'd insisted she hated until he gave it to her for Christmas sophomore year of high school and had worn ever since. He recognized her by the soft fur of the black winter boots Jackson had bought her for her 17th birthday, with a concealed heel to make her appear taller than the 5'2" she really was. He recognized her by the glint of the thin gold earrings in the shape of doves she'd bought with her first paycheck, back when she was sixteen and working at the drugstore downtown.

But little things had changed, he noticed, as his eyes adjusted and Aisha made her way to their table. The puffball on top of her olive hat was barely attached to the rest of the fabric, desperately clinging to it by three lonely strings. The laces in her boots had been pink when Jackson had given them to her. They were black now. Her earrings had dulled from the illustrious condition she normally worked so hard to keep them in, and she'd gotten helix's, Isaac realized with a start. From the first day he'd met her, Aisha had droned on and on about her desire for the double piercings in her upper ear cartilage, but she'd never had the guts to actually get them. That had changed, too.

"Hi, Isaac," she said softly, almost like she was apologizing, and he wondered what his face looked like to make her speak that way. He gestured for her to take a seat. There had been a time when Aisha slid into the seat across from him without asking, without saying hello, launching directly into a story or gossip from the day. Now she waited for his permission to sit. Isaac's stomach lurched.

"I'm glad you reached out," Aisha continued. She removed her hat and shoved it in her coat pocket, then shrugged off her coat and draped it over her chair. "I've been… everyone's been worried about you."

Isaac looked at the tiled floor, noting that the black and white checkered design was scuffed with winter sludge. "I'm okay."

"Ah," said Aisha. "I see."

For a moment she stared at him, and he knew what she saw. He was a little thinner than he used to be. The circles under his eyes had always been there, more or less, but they were darker now. And his hair was longer; he hadn't cut it since they'd seen each other last. Since the funeral.

"Isaac—"

"Aisha? The last time I saw you must've been a year ago!" Laila had caught sight of Aisha and grinned broadly as she made her way over to their table, the same one they'd sat in every week of high school. It was tucked in the back left corner of Drinks by Laila, next to a big, glass window with dark metal panes running through it. The window

3

was constantly foggy and looking through it made every-thing blurry, but to Isaac, the fog added a beautiful layer of mystique to the white flurries of snow billowing outside against the candy neon of the street's winter lights. The table itself was a rickety, wooden thing with the initials J A I scratched on the underside of it. It was surrounded by four of the least comfortable wooden chairs Isaac had ever sat in, but somehow, that never seemed to bother them. The chair to the left of Isaac's had been Jackson's. He tried not to look at it now.

"Sorry, Laila," Aisha said, blushing, but Isaac knew her well enough to know she was secretly extremely hap-py when Laila threw an arm around her shoulders and squeezed her close. Sure enough, when Laila pulled away, Aisha was blinking back tears. Aisha had been born with the pretty but massive blue eyes of a cartoon character, and when she teared up, the effect was magnified. If they'd still been friends, Isaac would have told her she looked like a bug. That's what he'd done when Aisha was sixteen and crying over her first heartbreak. The comment had shocked and offended her enough that her sobs had turned into hiccups which had eventually turned into laughter.

"Don't stay away so long next time! I missed you," said Laila. "My *sales* missed you," she added.

Aisha joined Laila's laughter. "I'll take a cup of your house coffee, please, Laila," Aisha said. "Better start mak-ing up that drop in revenue my absence has cost you."

Isaac nodded. "One for me, too. And she'll need extra

sugar." As soon as he'd said it, Isaac realized he had no idea if Aisha still added extra sugar to her coffee. He'd spoken immediately and instinctively, as if by muscle memory.

But Aisha snorted, conceding the point.

Laila frowned, then slowly started shaking her head. "Coffee? For you kids? Bad enough I've got Isaac in here every month, drinking a single black coffee and pretending he likes the taste. That's for grown-ups! What you kids need," she said, "is a cup of cocoa."

"Really, Laila—" started Aisha.

"We're not kids anymore—I'm twenty-one, Aisha's twenty-two—"

"If you want coffee, you're going to have to go someplace else. You're not getting it from me." Laila crossed her arms.

Isaac and Aisha locked eyes, and he shrugged. They knew when they were beaten. "We'll have the cocoa."

"Good idea," said Laila. As she and Aisha chatted about Laila's kids (Jayden was in seventh grade now, getting ready for his basketball tryouts, and Joshua was in fourth, learning to play oboe) and Aisha's new internship (it was a shame it wasn't paid, but then again, she was lucky to have any job opportunities in such a competitive city), Isaac was content to sit back and let the conversation flow over him, cocooning him in its soft blanket. After a while, Laila left their table, pausing along her way back to the drink counter to chat with a few other regulars.

Aisha smiled at Isaac, and for a second, it was like nothing had changed. "I missed her," she said.

Isaac glanced at the empty seat to his left.

"I miss him too," said Aisha hurriedly.

"You changed your shoelaces," Isaac responded.

Aisha swallowed. "I don't wear a lot of pink anymore," she said hoarsely. "They didn't match."

They stared at one another. Isaac crossed his arms.

"I tried to talk to you after the funeral," Aisha said. Her voice was stronger now. "I even went by your parents' house. No one answered."

"I have my own place downtown now," he said. "Across from that drugstore you used to work at."

Aisha looked at his face as if she was searching for something. "You should've told me. You should've called me back."

Isaac said nothing. How could he tell Aisha that for him, memories of Jackson and memories of Aisha were so intertwined as to be indistinguishable from one another? That seeing Aisha was like getting stabbed in the lung, that he was secretly glad she'd moved back to New York and stopped calling, that it had taken him six months of grief counseling to finally contact her because when he looked at her, he saw Jackson?

Jackson had always been funnier and more outgoing than him. At times Isaac had been jealous of all the attention Jackson got, but mostly he was grateful to have a best friend who made friends so easily. Jackson always had lots of friends. Too many friends, especially at college in Colorado. Friends who, unlike Issac, didn't keep track of how many drinks Jackson had or the last time he'd taken his diabetes medication. Friends that were too idiotic to consider that insulin shots turned alcohol, especially that much alcohol, into poison, and were too mind-numbingly stupid to understand that diabetic shock can be lethal if you don't get to the hospital in time. Or at all.

As much as Isaac had prided himself on being Jackson's best friend, when Jackson needed him most, he hadn't been there. Aisha always said Jackson needed to take better care of himself, that it wasn't Isaac's responsibility to look after him, but Isaac knew the truth: the only time it really mattered, he had failed.

"I still have them, you know," said Aisha, interrupting Isaac's thoughts. Her mouth was set into that stubborn jaw that would have been intimidating if he hadn't been eight inches taller than her. "The pink shoelaces. And the card he got me for my eighteenth birthday, the one that sings. And I know you're so wrapped up in your own misery that you can't possibly comprehend that someone else misses Jackson just as much as you do, but I kept his vinyl collection of Fall Out Boy records, too."

Isaac stared at Aisha, with her dull earrings and her old hat, and realized for the first time that she too had lost her best friend. His heart was fluttering, so weakly and so rapidly he thought it might give out. The coffee shop seemed to be spinning. Isaac set his hand on the scratched-up wooden table to steady himself and glanced outside to avoid Aisha's burning glare. The snow had stopped, but it was not a peaceful calm. It was a pause in the storm, as though the winter was holding its breath, ready to renew its attack with as much force as it could muster.

Thankfully, Laila returned to their table, dropping off two steaming hot mugs of cocoa in matching winter-themed mugs. Isaac's cup had a blue snowman on it. He took a deep inhale of the chocolate aroma of the drink and then a small sip and felt his chest loosen, ever so slightly.

"I'll pay," he said to Laila, but he was looking at Aisha.

"That's a funny way to say *I'm sorry*," Aisha responded, taking her own hot cocoa from Laila and nestling it between her hands. Her mug had a pattern of evergreen trees dusted in snow. "Can we get some cinnamon sticks for Isaac, please, Laila?" Aisha asked. Isaac found himself surprised that Aisha remembered his cocoa preferences. Then again, he'd remembered her coffee order.

Laila shook her head, reached into her apron, and pulled out a package of three small sticks of cinnamon. "You act like I don't know this boy. And here, honey, I brought you extra marshmallows. Just how you like it."

Aisha smiled. "You're the best, Laila."

"Got that right," Laila responded. "I've got some more drinks to make, but if you kids need anything else, just give me a holler." They promised they would.

Isaac watched Aisha pile marshmallow after marshmallow on top of her cocoa, until the brown liquid could no longer be seen, and felt the corner of his mouth twitch.

Aisha glanced up from her work. "You were apologiz-

8

ing," she prompted, as a gust of white wind smashed snow against the metal panes of the cloudy window. The storm had renewed, then. Aisha stacked another marshmallow on top of her pile hard enough that a bit of cocoa splashed outside of the mug. Isaac was afraid her marshmallow mountain would topple over, but Aisha didn't seem concerned as she reached for another. Suddenly, a memory popped into Isaac's head, and he was transported back to a time years before.

"Do you remember my sixteenth birthday?" he asked haltingly. "We were playing that game, where you see how many marshmallows you can fit in your mouth, and you fit 16. My record was 9."

"Chubby bunny," said Aisha, nodding. A smile flickered across her face. "I'm great at that game."

"And then you threw up after," said Isaac. He stirred his cocoa with a cinnamon stick. "And blamed it on my dog."

Aisha's eyes widened in outrage and she paused, marshmallow in hand. "That was because you had the brilliant idea to spend your birthday dinner trying gas station sushi because it was 'a third the price' and 'can't be that bad, really.'"

Isaac took a sip of his cocoa and closed his eyes briefly, appreciating the way the cinnamon and chocolate had fused together. "That was all Jackson's idea, actually."

"Oh, was it?" said Aisha, crossing her arms. "Okay. Well, remember winter break during freshman year of college, when you were going through your baking phase? And you entered that horrible bubblegum cheese pie into a baking contest, and you *won?* That was all Jackson, too. He voted like thirty-six times, and Courtney Hadish didn't stop him even though that was her *job* because she thought he was cute."

Isaac's mind was reeling. He'd thought that pie was pretty good. "Oh, so it's like that?" he said. He leaned forward as Aisha took a long drink of her cocoa, smearing marshmallow on her face. "Alright. You wanna know the only reason I stayed awake in any of your dance recitals? Jackson. Every time I'd doze off, he'd stab me in the leg with a pen. My thighs were covered in ink after every one."

"The reason Stacy Shumai asked you out junior year? Jackson."

"The reason I remembered your fifteenth, sixteenth, *and* seventeenth birthdays? Jackson."

Aisha's mouth dropped open. She whipped a marshmallow at him in indignation.

Isaac was so surprised, all he could do was blink as his brain tried to process what had just happened. The marshmallow, thrown with the force of significant aggravation and coated in a sticky layer of hot cocoa, clung to his cheek, slowly sliding downward and yet fighting valiantly to defeat gravity. After a moment, it lost the battle and dropped onto the table with a surprisingly wet *pop*. Issac wiped his face and stared at Aisha.

"S-sorry," she muttered, eyes wide. Her hands were over her mouth. "I didn't. . . . "

But whatever she didn't, Isaac never knew, because

10

he started laughing. Long, loud, heartfelt laughter. And because it felt good to laugh, and good to see Aisha laugh, he kept laughing, long after the joke had stopped being funny, until he was gasping for air and his eyes were running and his mouth hurt from forming a shape that had become unfamiliar to him.

Isaac was struck with a realization then, so shocking and yet so breathtakingly obvious he couldn't believe he hadn't seen it before: he had missed Aisha. He had missed her personality, a little bit sweet but a little bit acidic, and her ability to see through him that made him wonder why he bothered putting up a front at all, and everything else about her that had made her one of his best friends in the world. Jackson's memory hadn't killed his friendship with Aisha; it was his friendship with Aisha that was keeping Jackson's memory alive. She was the only other person in the world who had known Jackson, not the Jackson he pretended to be or the Jackson he thought he was, but Isaac's Jackson.

As Aisha recounted the story of Jackson's fifteenth birthday, when he'd ended up with green hair for four months because they'd mistakenly bought permanent dye, Isaac glanced out the corner of his eye to Jackson's vacant wooden chair. It didn't feel as empty as before. He could see, in his mind's eye, Jackson's figure leaning forward, arms pressed into the table, about to start a story that would have them all shooting their drinks out of their noses, wearing that awful green and orange sweater he'd insisted would be coming into fashion any day now. He could see Jackson, tipping the chair back as far as he could, precariously balanced on its back legs, until he inevitably went too far and crashed into the floor behind him. His expression had always been so comical; genuine shock mixed with a hint of betrayal, as though this time, he'd really thought it might work. Then, without fail, Laila would yell "Jackson!" and he would sheepishly sit up, promising never to do it again. Then, without fail, he would do it again.

Impulsively, Isaac reached out, across the table and their almost-empty mugs of cocoa and grabbed Aisha's hand. She stopped talking in surprise. After a moment, she squeezed his hand.

"I shouldn't have shut you out," Isaac said, swallowing. "I should have realized losing you *and* Jackson would be way worse than losing Jackson. And Aisha, I'm really... I mean, I'm really—"

"I know," she said, eyes bright. She gave a tight nod. "I know."

Isaac glanced again at the chair to his left, imagining he could see Jackson roll his eyes. *It's about time.*

"You're still here, Isaac," said Aisha. "Do you know that?"

Isaac looked down, at his fingers intertwined with Aisha's, and thought he could feel pleasant warmth spread from their linked hands up his arm to his entire body, easing the painful tightness in his chest and muscles of missing his best friend. Isaac faced Jackson's seat, and for the first time since his death, saw it for what it was: a wooden chair. Nothing more. He didn't imagine Jackson sitting in it; he didn't need to. Isaac returned his gaze to Aisha and nodded.

"It's not your fault, Isaac," Aisha said softly.

Isaac shrugged in response. Maybe Aisha was right—maybe Jackson's death hadn't been his fault, not entirely. But he wasn't ready to go down that path just yet. So instead they sat with their hands interlocked, sharing memories and enjoying one another's company, drinking their cocoa until it was long gone and the cups were cold.

Eventually, Aisha released his hand and stood, grabbing her coat. "I promised my mom I'd be back for dinner," she explained, threading her arms through the sleeves of her coat. Aisha fluffed her hair. "But I'll be in town for the rest of December and part of January. I want to see you again."

"It's pretty lonely to drink cocoa by yourself," Isaac said. Snow was falling lightly outside the window now, coating the gray pavement with its soft blanket. "I can keep you company."

"I'd like that."

"Excuse me?" said Laila, materializing at their table. She smacked down a handful of napkins. "I *know* you were not planning on leaving my coffee shop with the table looking like that."

Isaac blinked. He'd been so wrapped up in conversation that Aisha's cocoa spill and the fallen marshmallow had blended into the background of the tabletop. Under Laila's reproachful stare, the glossy cocoa reflected the outside lights twirling in the wind and the marshmallow shimmered silver against the wooden surface. Both were impossible to miss.

"Sorry, Laila," Isaac said, embarrassed, as he grabbed a napkin.

"Sorry, Laila," Aisha repeated, scrubbing alongside him.

"None of that," Laila said. She waved her arm as if to physically fan away the apology. "And Aisha, come back sooner next time, you hear?"

Aisha smiled and promised she would. The table now clean, she tossed down her napkin and reached in her pocket for her olive hat. As she pulled it out, the fabric snagged on her zipper. Aisha didn't seem to notice as she gave it a tug and with an impossibly loud *snap*, the three brave strings holding the puffball to her hat finally ripped. Aisha looked down at the carnage: the puffball, cradled tenderly in her hand, and the hat, still wedged in her pocket. She bit her lip and blinked furiously.

"Laila, is that sewing kit still behind the counter?" Isaac blurted. "The one that Jackson left here when he was practicing stitching in one of his pre-med classes freshman year?"

"Oh, my," said Laila. "I'd forgotten about that. Sure is. I'll go get it; you kids just—wait right here." Laila gave Isaac's shoulder a brief squeeze, then bustled away. Isaac

14

and Aisha looked at one another, silently agreeing to pretend they hadn't noticed Laila wipe her eyes as soon as she'd turned around.

Aisha cleared her throat. Her eyes were bright. "Isaac, I appreciate the sentiment, but a sewing kit is only helpful if you know how to sew," she said. "I don't."

"I do," Isaac replied. "I can reattach the puffball to the hat, if you want. It won't be like it's brand-new, not exactly, but it'll be good. Stronger."

Aisha slid back into her seat and offered him the hat. "I'd like that. A lot," she sniffled, voice small.

"You look like a bug," he responded. "Do you have to cry about everything?"

And when she laughed, Isaac thought for the first time in almost a year that someday, he might be okay.

•• [2] ••

THE PRINCESS AND THE WITCH

Once upon a time, there lived a gorgeous and kind princess and a prince who were madly in love. One day, the prince proposed. Overcome with joy, she agreed to marry him in one week's time at sunset.

The gorgeous and kind princess kissed the prince goodnight and went to sleep in her private chambers. She awoke at dawn and went to wish her true love a good morning, but when she reached the guest chambers in which he had been sleeping, she found them empty. The prince had vanished. Distraught, the gorgeous and kind princess sent out her soldiers in search of him, knowing the prince would never willingly leave her, but it was in vain. The prince, her true love, was gone.

She did not give up. The gorgeous and kind princess worked tirelessly for six days and six nights, yet she could not determine where her true love had been taken. On the dawn of the seventh day, desperate, she approached a witch living in a small stone cottage a few hours from the castle. Surrounding the cottage was a field of yellow grass and a few small, twisted trees.

Taking a breath, she clutched her gown in one hand and knocked on the wooden door with the other.

"Greetings, my dear," said the witch as she creaked open the door. She was a gaunt old woman dressed in rags. "What is it you desire?"

"I need to find my true love, the prince," the gorgeous and kind princess said. "He has been taken from me."

"Of course," said the witch, and ushered her inside. They sat at the witch's kitchen table, upon which rested a single bowl containing a gel-like substance. "I can give you a magic map, which will lead directly towards him," the witch said, "but I will need something in return."

The gorgeous and kind princess nodded; she had expected as much. "Whatever the price, I will pay it."

"Your beauty," said the witch. "Give me your grace, your poise. Give me your youth and the blood that pulses so vibrantly beneath your skin. Give me the shine in your hair and the sparkle in your eyes and the confident beating of your heart within your chest."

The gorgeous and kind princess bit her lip. She touched a hand to her face, feeling the smooth skin. How often she had taken her long lashes and pink lips for granted. Still, she knew her love was not superficial and worth much more than a pretty face. The two women shook and the deal was done.

The witch grabbed her arm. Stunned, the kind princess watched the color and elasticity flow from her skin to the witch's; while her own arm withered and grew weak, the witch's became strong and smooth. The kind princess's gaze continued upward, landing on the witch's face. She was startled to find her reflection staring back at her. The kind princess glanced down at the bowl on the table and saw a hallowed, plain face swimming in the gel, blinking when she blinked. Her heart twisted, but she remained steadfast in her decision; this would reunite her with her true love.

The witch smiled and examined her new hand, admiring the tautness of the skin. She snapped and a map materialized. "This dot is your prince," said the witch, pointing on the map. "It will move as he does; follow it and you will find him."

The kind princess grabbed the map, surprised to learn that the prince had been hidden in the chapel where they had intended to wed. The kind princess rushed out of the cottage, but when she arrived at the chapel, she discovered it was encircled by a large gate. The height of its iron spikes taunted her. The kind princess grabbed the gate and shook, but it remained sturdy. It was far too tall for her to climb over. There was no one else around. She considered making the trek back to the castle, but quickly decided against it; it was a long journey and she feared for the safety of the prince. Still, she could not bear to give up with her true love so near.

Frustrated, she returned to the cottage in the woods and banged on the door. She hissed at the pain that spiked up from her weak arm.

"Welcome, my dear," the witch said as she pulled open the door. "What is it you desire?"

"I need a way into the chapel," said the kind princess.

Nodding, the witch allowed her to enter. They sat at the table. "I can give you this, but I will need something in return."

The kind princess took a breath. "I am prepared."

"Your reputation," said the witch. "Give me your title, your crown. Pass on the cage of expectation and the weight of perception. I want the status you hold and the power you wield and the image of who others claim you to be."

The kind princess hesitated to give up her kingdom. She was confident it would prosper even without her, but love of her position made her pause. The kind princess tucked a strand of dry, dead hair behind her ear. It was a difficult choice, but she knew success without love was nothing. In the end, love of her prince won. The two women shook and the deal was done.

A strong wind blasted throughout the cottage, making the window quiver and the kettles shake. The kind princess squeezed her eyes shut against it and felt it bite her wilted skin. As the wind died, she opened her eyes and saw that the beautiful red gown and sparkling silver crown that had once belonged to the princess and the gray rags that had once belonged to the witch were reversed.

The witch inhaled deeply. The corner of her mouth twitched upward. Then she snapped her fingers crisply and a key appeared. "This will allow you to open the gate," she said.

The kind woman clasped the key tightly to her chest and began the walk back to the chapel. The journey was long and slow-going; having made the trip twice already that day without the aid of youth, the kind woman was exhausted. Still, she had the perseverance of love, and pressed onwards.

The kind woman arrived at the chapel, twisted the key in the gate, and quickly walked inside. She took out her map and peered closely at the dot that was her true love. Pulling open the doors to the sanctuary, she found the prince slumped on the floor. The kind woman rushed down the aisle between the pews and crouched over him. His chest neither rose nor fell and fear strangled her heart.

"Wake," she begged, shaking his arm. "Wake."

He did not.

The kind woman stayed there for hours, sobbing. A warm, dusk glow illuminated the sanctuary and the kind woman realized it was a mere hour from sunset, when they would have been wed. She found new resolve in that fact; a wedding she was promised and a wedding she would have. Her old bones cracked as she rose. She grabbed the prince's cold legs and dragged his body out of the sanctuary. The kind woman's frail arms quivered with the strain, but she continued, determined to tow him all the way to the witch's cottage.

As the kind woman heaved open the sanctuary door, she was greeted by the witch. The kind woman froze. Her heart fluttered rapidly. The soft hair, the sparkling crown, the red dress; the witch appeared exactly as the kind woman knew she had once looked. The comparison stole the breath from her lungs. The kind woman felt an ache pierce her ribs as she was confronted with all she had given away.

"Hello, my dear," said the witch. It hurt the kind woman to hear the melodic tone in the witch's voice. "I heard you crying."

"I need a way to bring back my love," said the kind woman hoarsely but without preamble.

The witch nodded, as though she had been expecting the request, and looked at her through beautiful dark lashes. "That is no easy task," she responded, stepping inside the sanctuary and closing the door. "I will ask a great price."

"What is it you desire?" asked the kind woman.

"Your heart," said the witch. "Give me your laughter, your love. Give me the softness with which you gaze upon your beloved and the smile you save for his name. I want the dreams you hold dear and iron in your spine and the passion that burns within your chest."

22

The kind woman swallowed and became aware of how deeply tired she felt. To give up that much of herself would be truly a hardship. Without her heart, would she still know her prince? Yet, if she did not make the trade, her true love would never wake. She had come too far and given up too much to forfeit now. The two women shook and the deal was done.

The kind woman felt an invisible fist squeeze her heart; tighter, tighter. She doubled over, gasping for air. Just when she was sure death was imminent, the fist receded, taking the pain with it. The woman now felt nothing at all and straightened slowly. The witch too was breathing hard, clutching her chest. Noticing the woman's gaze, the witch snapped her fingers and a vial appeared, full of a golden liquid. Dazed, the woman reached for it, but the witch shook her head.

"His life is too delicate," she said. "I must administer it myself."

Nodding, the woman ushered the witch to the lifeless corpse on the floor. The witch bent over him, poured the drink down his throat, and spoke softly. As she chanted, the liquid began to glow, until it was so bright it could be seen running through the prince's veins, the glittering gold stark against his dark skin. The witch ceased speaking and all was still. The golden glow of the liquid faded and faded until it was gone. Suddenly, the prince's eyes flew open and he gasped for air.

"My love," he said, staring in wonderment at the witch.

23

"Let us be wed," responded the witch, helping him stand. The prince winced as he was pulled to his feet, gingerly touching the back of his head.

"The ceremony is minutes away," the witch continued. "We must go to the altar."

"No," the woman said after a moment.

The prince wrenched his gaze from the witch, noticing the woman for the first time.

"This witch is trying to trick you," the woman explained. "She is merely an impostor of your true love."

The prince frowned and looked to the witch, who stared lovingly back into his eyes. "Look at my face, my crown, my smile. I *am* your true love."

The prince's frown softened into a smile and he grabbed the witch's hand.

Mutely, the woman shook her head. The prince turned back to her, sympathetic.

"She has the appearance of my love, the reputation of my love, and the heart of my love," he said. "What is left?"

"Sacrifice."

"Why, that is nothing at all."

"What of my love?" persisted the woman. "I have given up everything to save you."

"Who are you?" responded the prince, and the woman realized she did not know.

"Come, my love," said the witch. She snapped her fingers and the sanctuary doors opened, revealing a small congregation. The prince joined her at the altar as the wedding march began to play. The gathered guests looked on as vows were exchanged and the two were wed.

Clutching her rags about her, the gaunt old woman watched the wedding party pass.

AUTHOR'S NOTE

"The Princess and the Witch" is not a love story. It's a fairytale about identity and sacrifice.

An attentive reader might have noticed that as the piece progresses and the gorgeous and kind princess gives up more and more of herself, she loses parts of her identity. She becomes the kind princess, then the kind woman, and finally the woman. In fact, the descriptions and dialogue of the princess and the witch reverse completely over the course of the story.

I wanted to write a fairytale because the form allows for the simplification of complex ideas; plot and moral hold the piece together. "The Princess and the Witch" is designed to make the reader question who the prince's true love is and, more generally, how much of an identity can be altered before it is replaced.

TIPS ON THE CARE AND UPKEEP OF

THE EVER-ELUSIVE "GIRLFRIEND"

As all friend-zoned people and "nice guys" know, getting a girlfriend is not an easy task. Luckily, through research conducted across multiple genders and sexualities, I have compiled data detailing how to ask out and maintain a girlfriend for maximum wifey results.

Before any maintaining of a girlfriend can be discussed, you must have a girlfriend to maintain. Asking a girl out is no easy task. It must be undertaken with surgical precision; exactly the right mix of jokes (enough for her to know you're funny, but not enough for her to get annoyed), compliments (enough for her to know you're interested, but not enough for it to be creepy), and actual conversation (enough for her to know who you are, but not enough to overpower her voice). You must be confident but not cocky, vulnerable but not pathetic, and above all, you must have It. There is not a single thing more important to a potential girlfriend than whether or not you have It. This ambiguous yet necessary quality is the boundary line between funny and annoying. It is what separates the complimenters from the creeps. Quite frankly, if you do not have It, your odds of successfully asking a girl out dwindle exponentially the more she realizes the quality you lack.

THE TIPS:

1. Once you have acquired your girlfriend, the first thing you must do in order to satisfy this wonderful person is, of course, to keep her well-fed. I cannot stress the importance of this enough. Girlfriends are notoriously less agreeable when hungry. At least eighty percent of arguments can be resolved through the offering of good food, and the twenty percent that cannot be resolved by it can at least be briefly pacified by its presence.

2. The second and equally important thing you must do is support her. Girlfriends are creatures often lacking in support (why do you think they wear bras?). It is your responsibility to provide her with as much support as you can give. Her dreams are your dreams; her successes are your successes. I have included a few examples of how to support your girlfriend below:

2a. If she receives a promotion at work, it would be appropriate to throw a feast in her honor. Or at least take her out to dinner.

2b. On her birthday, present her with a sweet dessert lit on fire, stand in a circle around her with all her close friends and family, and begin the traditional chant. You must also prepare a small offering in her honor on this day.

2c. If she is upset, I must refer you to tip #1. Perhaps sending her videos of baby animals would help.

3. Third: reciprocate. You know what I'm talking about.

4. Fourth, you must provide her with unlimited attention. Let her know you care; express your love for her and your genuine pleasure at her existence. Respond to her texts before she sends them. She is a delight in your life and should be treated as such. However, girlfriends are not unreasonable; a brief break from attention-giving can be typically negotiated to take place during your standard sleeping hours. If you are not currently giving your girlfriend attention, please apologize and begin doing so immediately.

5. Fifth and final, if you're not rich, get rich. Getting a girlfriend is a very poor choice if your goal is to save money. The following list of dates is known to increase happiness in girlfriends by at least 6.9 percent:

5a. Concert tickets. Do not simply buy her mosh pit tickets to one concert; rather, purchase backstage passes to every concert that particular artist has ever and will ever perform. This will let her know you remember little details about her, such as her favorite band.

5b. Take her on a shopping spree. She should of course have access to your credit card, retirement fund, and social security number at all times. Even if she doesn't like shopping for clothes, there are other things guaranteed to please her, such as yachts. Remember, if you have $20 and your girlfriend has $5, your girlfriend has $25.

5c. Throw caviar at the homes of her enemies. This conveys the same intent as TP-ing a house, but the caviar serves as a reminder that you are much wealthier and therefore happier and more committed than they will ever be. Your girlfriend will love that you are willing to fight for her and see this as a testament to your loyalty.

I hope these tips are beneficial to you as you begin your time-honored search for a "wifey." Remember that although this list seems daunting, the rewards of attaining a girlfriend are limitless and the endeavor is well worth your while. Good luck and Godspeed.

•• [4] ••

A WALK IN THE PARK

There once lived a warrior, protected by the most powerful armor in all the land.

The warrior prized his armor. Each day he shined it lovingly until he could see the reflection of the sky in the beautiful, silvery metal. It became who he was. Occasionally, a weapon would find a chink in the armor, causing him searing pain, but the warrior would dress the wound and fortify the armor until it was twice as strong as before.

In fact, this armor was so strong that when the warrior was seventeen and Cupid tried to shoot an arrow into his heart, it merely got stuck halfway inside his breastplate.

Oliver tried to concentrate on his math homework. Mia, the pretty girl who sat in the seat diagonal to his, was leaning back in her silver metal chair, looking at him again. He'd caught her staring twice this period already as she pretended to analyze the unit circle poster on the yellow brick wall behind him.

"You're staring at me," Oliver finally stated, glancing up from his assignment. For some reason, the fact that Mia smelled like peppermint was making it difficult for him to focus on calculating tangents.

"I am not," responded Mia. She quickly scanned the room, but most of the other students in their pre-calculus class were asleep or listening to music as they worked.

"You are," said Oliver. He put his pencil down on the scratched, wooden desk he sat at and leaned towards Mia, locking eyes. "See? You're doing it right now."

She laughed, and Oliver felt a smile tugging at his own mouth. From the desk to his left, Andre, Oliver's best friend, made a strangled coughing noise that sounded remarkably similar to *shut up*.

"You're cute," Mia said, either not hearing Andre's comment or simply choosing to ignore him. She grabbed the corner of Oliver's paper and scribbled down some numbers. "Call me sometime," she said. "If you need someone to study with."

"Maybe I will," he said as the bell rang. Students zipped their backpacks shut, sounding like a hive of bees, and bolted toward the door.

Mia swung her backpack over her shoulder and smiled at Oliver, a hypnotizing smile that made him admire the warmth in her brown eyes. "Maybe I'll talk to you later, then."

Oliver watched her walk out the door. Immediately after it closed behind her, Andre turned to face him.

"Are you dumb?" he asked, crossing his arms.

Oliver blinked, then shrugged. "Probably," he admitted. "Why?"

"You'd better call her."

"Andre—"

"I'm serious, Oliver." Andre shook his head. "Her dad coaches varsity, and you know we're both trying out for soccer next month. Do not blow this for us."

"Yeah," said Oliver, rubbing the bridge of his nose. "Yeah. I'll call her."

Unbeknown to the warrior, the arrow Cupid had shot into his breastplate was tipped in poison and it began to weaken his beautiful, strong, almost-impenetrable armor. As the arrow wormed its way deeper and deeper into his chest, the warrior was surprised to feel the sense of something, like the echo of an emotion. He wondered what it would be like to be happy.

As time wore on, more and more of his armor flaked away. The warrior looked down at the crumbling gray metal and removed the rest of it himself, piece by piece, until all that remained was the solitary arrow lodged in his heart. He was more vulnerable this way, but without the crushing weight of the metal, he found himself much more free.

"I'll take a medium rocky road and a date this Friday," said Oliver, walking up to the counter of the ice cream shop where Mia worked. Oliver, wearing a gray jacket over a black t-shirt depicting the death of a star, felt a little out of place in the baby blue and cotton candy pink aesthetic of the building. Mia, on the other hand, with her sweet, soft smile and clean white apron, fit right in.

"I happen to know you have a six month anniversary dinner planned for this Friday," she said, playing along.

"Maybe I'll see you there."

"Maybe you will."

Mia entered Oliver's ice cream order on the cash register. As he waited for his dessert, a gust of chilly air swept through the shop, and Oliver glanced toward the glass doors, annoyed. In walked a young woman with dark circles under her eyes, pulling a frayed red scarf over her nose. Clutching her hand, in a dirty pink coat and a hat that was clearly made for an adult, was her child, who couldn't have been more than three years old. They ordered two hot dogs from Mia.

"And I want an ice cream," the girl said. "A big one. With chocolate."

Mia laughed and began to type in the order.

"No, I'm sorry," said the mother in a low voice. "Cancel that. Alissa, sweetie, what have I told you about ordering without asking mommy? We don't have money for that today."

The little girl's face fell. She puffed out her bottom lip.

"Lucky for you," said Mia brightly, "little girls named Alissa get free ice cream today! I'll make yours myself."

And she did.

Oliver sat within the pastel hues of the ice cream shop, enjoying the almond crunch in his chocolate dessert, waiting for the mother and daughter to leave. When they had gone, he stood, dropped his empty ice cream bowl in the trash, and approached the counter. "Why did you do that?" he asked Mia, genuinely curious. He wouldn't have done the same.

"Why wouldn't I?" Mia responded. She laughed a little, as if the question confused her.

That was the first time Oliver thought that he loved her. But he knew what those words meant, what saying them would cause, so he closed his mouth and let the moment slip away.

One day, Cupid visited the warrior again. She reached out and touched the arrow she had shot in the warrior's chest, noticed it was embedded in his flesh, noticed the lack of armor. Cupid nodded, satisfied, and ripped the arrow from his heart.

The pain was unbearable. The warrior watched his life bleed out and began to heave. He reached out blindly for his armor—his beautiful, strong armor—but it was gone. Cupid was cruel now and stabbed him again and again in the chest. Perhaps she was dissatisfied with his treatment of the arrow; perhaps she felt it deserved a more welcoming host, someone with less trauma and more light. Perhaps she thought he had not been thankful enough for her arrow, destroying the armor he had once loved. Maybe the warrior had been too greedy, too careless. Perhaps the price of using love as a savior was having to watch it die on the cross.

Cupid, her work done, turned to leave, to return to the above and leave him to die.

"How long," the warrior gasped. He reached out, praying she understood. Cupid turned to him.

"As long as it takes," she said, in a rich and quiet voice. "As long as it takes."

Oliver parked his gray sedan outside Mia's green stucco house and faced her. She'd been unusually quiet during the ride back—the type of quiet that he knew meant she was thinking a million things at once. Mia knotted her hands in her hair. "Why did you introduce me as your classmate?" she eventually asked.

Oliver sighed. He'd known she was upset about that the moment he'd said it. "I just don't want them to know yet, Mia." They'd had this conversation many times before.

"Not again," she said, shaking her head. "You cannot tell me you're just not ready for your family to know about us again. It's been nine months, Oliver. You've met my whole family on multiple occasions and I finally have dinner with yours and I'm your *classmate?*"

Oliver shrugged, unable to express how much she meant to him. Mia's comment wasn't entirely fair—Mia's dad had been Oliver's soccer coach; of course they'd spent time together. Still, Oliver wished he had something better to offer her.

"Are you ashamed of me? Is that it?" asked Mia, turning to look at him. The tip of her nose was red.

"No, Mia," Oliver said. He reached for Mia's hand but she snatched it away.

"Then what is it?" she asked, voice rising. "How come you never say *I love you*, Oliver? You just say *love you* or *you too*. It's not the same. It doesn't mean the same."

Before he could protest, Mia continued. "And I cannot believe you didn't tell me about your mom, Oliver. I cannot believe you let me ask your family if she'd be joining us for dinner as if you didn't know she hadn't eaten dinner with you in four years. I cannot—" Mia's voice broke. "Oliver, do you even like me?"

And Oliver tried. He really did. The words got all the way up his throat to the tip of his tongue before his mouth slammed shut and trapped them inside. He shrugged again, helplessly.

"Oliver, I can't do this!" Mia yelled. Her tears glowed with the reflection of a nearby streetlamp. "I need a boy-friend who can communicate and who trusts me and I don't think you'll ever trust me. And if that's true, if that's never going to be you, then you need to tell me right now because *I can't handle this!*" She slammed her hand down on her thigh.

Oliver was silent for a moment. His throat was tight; his seatbelt seemed to be suffocating him.

"It's not me," he said finally. Oliver ran a hand across his face. He wished he was lying.

"Okay," said Mia, voice high and raspy. She looked out the smudgy car window and wiped her eyes. "Okay."

The warrior lay on the battlefield, bleeding out.

Seconds and minutes and hours he laid there, in agony, staring up at the sky as it turned orange and then pink and then darkened into night. The warrior tried to drift off to sleep, hoping for it to ease the pain, but he was cold; the ground, uncomfortable. Besides, it was too light to sleep. He opened his eyes, staring straight up, and saw the stars. And within them, the warrior found something unexpected: beauty.

Beauty was in the soft glow of the stars as they twinkled

and danced in the sky. It was in the shine of the moon, maternally looking after all its children. It was in the harmony between the planets and the constellations and the twists in the galaxy. As he realized this, the warrior realized there was beauty in his soul, too. We are all only stardust.

With this revelation came another; strength was present in the way the stars sparkled in the sky at night, having been thoroughly defeated each day. It was there in the way the moon waxed and waned in a constant state of change but never faltered. He found strength in his spirit, battered as it was, because it too fought and would continue to fight until the end of forever and then perhaps a little bit more.

Realizing this, the warrior's chest began to warm, and for a second he was afraid another bout of agonizing pain would follow, but as the soothing heat spread from his heart to his head and his toes he relaxed and let it flow through him, easing his aches and pains, stitching his bloody chest back together. Then, as day came and the warmth in his chest abated, he propped himself up on his elbow and rose jerkily to a stand.

"I heard about what happened," Andre said, opening the door to Oliver's bedroom and leaning against a wall decorated floor to ceiling with science posters and newspaper clippings. It didn't surprise Oliver that Andre had entered his house without Oliver's invitation; Andre had known the garage code since they were twelve and came over more or less whenever he wanted. Oliver paused the documentary about hermit crabs he was watching, grabbed a handful of popcorn, and looked up at Andre expectantly.

"Mia told me."

Oliver's stomach felt like it was fighting an epic battle against the popcorn he'd just swallowed. "What did she say? Did she tell you why?"

Andre nodded and crossed his arms. "Look, Oliver . . . you know I've got your back, 100%, but . . . man, the only reason I know anything about your life is because I've lived it with you. You think you would've told me about the night your mom packed her bags and promised to come back but never did if I hadn't been there? How about before that, when your dad cheated on her with his accountant? Give me a break." Andre snorted. "We've been best friends since what, second grade? And you still don't talk to me. I mean, just look at today—I heard about the breakup from Mia, not you. I get it, Oliver, I really do. But she just wanted to get to know you, man. Maybe that's not such a bad thing."

Oliver smiled sardonically and hurled the TV remote at Andre. Andre caught the remote, almost as if he'd anticipated the movement, and tossed it lightly back on the bed. "Yeah, yeah, I know," Andre said. "But somebody had to say it."

Oliver looked away. He clenched his fists in his navy

quilt and twisted the fabric. "I'm sick of people leaving," he muttered, forcing the words out of his mouth.

"Ten years and I'm still here," said Andre, pushing off the wall to sit on the bed beside him. "So is your dad, and your sister, and your cat. That has to count for something."

Oliver glared at him. "You're saying it's all in my head."

"Isn't that where you keep your thoughts? Where else would it be, idiot?" Andre asked, reaching behind Oliver to smack him on the back of the head. "I'm saying I'm sorry your mom left, I really am, and I'm sorry your dad destroyed your faith in love or whatever, but you don't have to repeat their mistakes. You can choose to trust people anyway."

Oliver nodded slightly and offered Andre some popcorn. As the two finished the documentary, Andre's words echoed in Oliver's head.

As the warrior prepared to cross the battlefield once more, he considered crafting more armor. He could see it now: beautiful, strong, impenetrable. Nothing would be able to touch him.

And yet . . . the warrior liked feeling the wind tousle his hair, liked smelling campfires in the summer, liked hearing birds sing. He remembered the crushing weight of his past burden and decided he would accept all wounds acquired in crossing without protection.

Step by step, the warrior walked across the battlefield, tensed, waiting to die. Yet there was neither the clash of a sword nor the boom of a bullet. It was quiet—peaceful, almost. Why hadn't he seen the dazzling shades of green in the crisp grass before? This scenic park—for that was what it was, certainly no battle had ever been fought here—was gorgeous. Why had he never noticed the way the clouds kiss the horizon as the sun rests in the sky? The warrior did not want to be invincible; he wanted to be vulnerable, wanted to be able to get hurt. He accepted the scratches and even broken ribs he might acquire in the future and with one foot in front of the other, crossing alone but standing tall, he began to smile.

•• [5] ••

Rust

It wasn't that I could sense it—I mean, the clock on the wall should have chimed exactly at my third knock on her door like it did every day at 4pm when I came to deliver her mail, it should have but it didn't and, I don't know, I guess I just didn't realize. That's how we met, Annie and I; I dropped off her mail and she was always so sweet and so beautiful, inviting me in for tea except when it was cider.

So I'm waiting on the front steps for her to let me in and now I'm tapping my feet (tap tap tap) and, you know, it's kind of funny but Annie hasn't answered the door yet. I start pacing back and forth on the steps (one two three turn one two three turn) over and over and over until she answers except that she doesn't answer. I don't know what to do so I decide to knock on her door (knock knock knock pause knock knock knock) and I keep doing that until her clock should have chimed again, it should have but it didn't. At this point I start to think something is wrong so I try the door handle and it's unlocked so I let myself in.

The first thing I notice is—well, it's not a big thing, it's just that—Annie always takes her shoes off when she gets home, they're always stacked neatly to the left of her welcome mat (90 degrees to the left). She likes tiny compact shoes and she likes them black and she takes them off to the left except today I notice they're off to the right. And not clean, either, not at 90 degree angles like she likes (like I like) but instead just kind of, I don't know, strewn about.

One looks like it's been kind of haphazardly kicked off over there by the carpet and it's not a big deal but, well, there's a stain on her nice white carpet and it doesn't really look like dirt but I'm worried it will set so I take off my shoes (90 degrees to the left) and I go to her kitchen (it's just past the bathroom on the right) and grab some cleaner and a towel and go back to her carpet with her haphazard shoes but before I do I notice a cup of tea sitting on the kitchen counter and I think that's weird, Annie drinks coffee, but I drink tea so I taste it and it's cold and I don't drink it cold so I go back to the carpet by her welcome mat and start scrubbing.

The stain looks like maybe it's been there for awhile because I'm scrubbing and scrubbing and it kind of smells

44

like metal and it's not coming out it's just adding rust to the towel but I can't exactly stop, see, because she has such a nice white carpet so I just scrub two three scrub two three scrub two three and by the time I get it out her clock should have chimed (it should have but it didn't). So I put away her cleaning supplies and I pick up her shoes and put them to the left of her welcome mat (90 degrees, 90 degrees) and take a look around because she's still not there.

I guess I should have seen it earlier—I should have but I didn't—her clock was broken. It had fallen off the wall where I had so carefully mounted it for her (she had nitpicked about having it hung just so but I told her I liked nitpicking and isn't it better, anyway, if it's exactly centered above the desk?). There's a big scratch in the paint on the wall and I have to clean it but I don't know how to clean it so I start pacing, one two three turn one two three turn, until I can think of what to do but I can't think because my mind is going one two three turn where is she where is she one two three.

Her bedroom! She's probably in her bedroom. She probably fell asleep after her shift at the hospital today and now she's asleep in her bedroom. I walk over to her bedroom (it's the first door on the left) but when I reach the door there's another one of those stains, the almost-mud-but-it's-not-mud stains, and the smell of iron is really strong here so I go back to the kitchen and grab her cleaning supplies and her towel and I see that horrible awful terrible picture she has on her fridge, that one of

45

her with the tall man with the shaded eyes. So anyway I go back to the carpet just outside her bedroom and I scrub two three scrub two three scrub two three until the rust lifts and I know her clock should have chimed. It should have but it didn't.

I figure I probably should hold on to the cleaning supplies and the towel so I knock on her bedroom door (knock knock knock pause knock knock knock) and wait for her to open it for me except she doesn't open it for me. So finally I just open it myself and go in and I notice there's a lot more stains here, all over her nice white carpet, kind of like a trail, I guess, like a trail. And I feel like I'm about to throw up because that metallic smell is stuck inside my brain but of course I can't not clean it so I crouch back down on the floor but as I crouch down on the floor I can see underneath her bed and I can see my reflection in her eyes and I laugh because why is she being so silly, it's much more comfortable on top of the bed, everyone knows that.

So I say, "Annie, what are you doing? You should be up there." She really should be up there it's much more comfortable but she doesn't seem to agree with me, she doesn't really say anything, actually, but Annie's a quiet girl so I ask if I can lift her up and when she doesn't say anything again I start to get a little angry so I grab her arm and shake.

"Can I lift you up? Can I lift you up?" I ask, and of course she doesn't answer, and I start to think how that's not like Annie not like Annie at all but now I'm getting kind of nervous and my reflection in her eyes looks a little scared.

I take her arm and start to pull but she's all dead weight so I heave and heave and when I switch my grip to her waist my hands are covered in that rust, too, like the floor like the trail on the floor, but I yank and pull and twist and heave until she's on the bed and that's when I see how maybe all the rust in the house came from her stomach and her leg and her head and I think oh no oh no oh no.

I try to wake her up ("Annie! Annie! Annie!") but she doesn't want to wake up and I can't breathe it's only inhaling no exhaling I can't see why can't I see and I think I'm sitting but maybe I'm falling and I can't see I can't see I can't see and I'm rocking back and forth and back and forth and trying to count (one two three one two three) but my mouth keeps saying "Annie Annie Annie" over and over and over and her clock should have chimed again it really should have God it should have but it didn't so I just keep rocking and rocking and rocking and eventually when it should have chimed again I realize my eyes are closed so I open them and take a breath (I can breathe again) and I go stand by Annie, my beautiful Annie, but there's so much rust I have to start cleaning so I grab my towel and her leg and it's scrub two three scrub two three scrub two

BAM.

The door flies open and I freeze and I can't breathe

(I never could) and the man walks closer and closer and closer. He's so big and he's so strong "suspect" he says and "questioning" he adds what does that mean what does that mean (one two one two) there is metal on my wrists (one two one two) and I know I should have moved I know I should have talked (I know I should have).

But I didn't.

AUTHOR'S NOTE

If I did my job right, you might need to take a relaxing breath after reading that piece. I wanted to create something bursting with tension containing very little gore and one big unanswered question.

Whether or not the narrator killed Annie is up to each reader's personal interpretation. Annie's "hospital" shift could be in a psychiatric ward; perhaps the narrator is a patient who imagined a relationship with his nurse, visited her in her home, and reacted violently to a picture of her husband on the fridge. When Annie told the narrator she wanted exclusively a professional relationship with him and that any other insinuation was outside reality, he could have killed her in blind rage. Perhaps he wasn't even aware death would be the consequence of his actions. There is nothing aside from the narrator's word that proves Annie takes her shoes off to the left or that any knowlege the narrator claims to have of Annie is accurate. Maybe he was only in the house to clean up the evidence of murder;

the cup of cold tea could be a sign that he'd been in her home earlier that day.

However, maybe the narrator really was a friendly mailman and he and Annie were close friends or even lovers. Perhaps the narrator's desire to clean the blood or his anxious ramblings were his reaction to or denial of the knowledge that a violent crime had been committed on someone he cared for. The picture on Annie's fridge could be an image of her and her brother, and the narrator's hatred of it could stem from his hatred of her brother or even that it was *that* unflattering. Maybe the picture is of Annie's ex-boyfriend who mistreated her, so the narrator despises him and therefore the image on Annie's behalf. The cup of cold tea could have been prepared by Annie, awaiting the narrator's arrival for their daily chats. The intimate knowledge the narrator has of Annie, such as her shoe habits, proves the closeness of their friendship.

Was the narrator kind, checking in on someone he cares for, or suspicious, removing the evidence of murder?

That's the beauty of an unreliable narrator; I write the words, but the reader tells the story.

•• [6] ••

IT STARTED WITH LIGHT

Lucifer ran his fingers through his soft, dark hair, knowing that no matter how many times he messed it up, it would always fall perfectly back into place. He smoothed his already-smooth suit and straightened his perfectly straight tie. Lucifer reached into his pocket and pulled out a pair of black, square-rimmed sunglasses he used to dim the eternal fire that smoldered in his eye sockets. He put them on and took a deep breath.

"You look good," said Michael, exasperated. Michael was an archangel, unlike Lucifer, who was only an angel, and had a much different sense of fashion. While Lucifer preferred to adopt a human form, mimicking the bodies and styles of those he served, Michael enjoyed merging human and animal characteristics. Currently, he had fused the body of a man with aspects of a swan and a lion, creating a slightly terrifying humanoid form with wings, a tail, and a light brown mane of human hair. As an archangel, he also wore a crown of pure light. The halo was a coveted symbol in Heaven and Michael wore it with pride. He grabbed Lucifer's arm. "We need to get moving if we're going to make it through Purgatory in time for your promotion."

"It's not necessarily a promotion, Michael. You know how summons are," Lucifer protested, trying to banish his smile. He appreciated his best friend's optimism, though he couldn't quite share it. Lucifer followed Michael through a small gate into an infinite garden, full of fruits and vegetables and souls—lots and lots of souls. Their human-shaped forms of light were difficult to look at, even for an angel like himself. In his peripheral vision, they shone vividly, vibrant with the memory of life. Looking straight on, they seemed to disappear, as though suddenly realizing they were only an echo. Only by concentrating very intently could Lucifer depict the color of one's eyes or the shape of another's nose. Though souls were challenging to see and had no real physical form, it was still considered extremely rude to pass through them and Lucifer did his best to avoid it.

As they walked through Purgatory, he let his mind wander. The truth was, Lucifer had been a shoo-in for archangel for the last two thousand years. He answered more prayers than any other beings, archangel or otherwise. His clients always walked away with what they wanted. Sometimes, in severe cases, Lucifer would even temporarily possess the body of the human to fix the problem himself. Why he had not previously been made an archangel was beyond him.

Michael ushered spirits to the side as they crunched over some strawberry bushes. "Whose idea was Purgatory, anyway?" he muttered. "The doors to Judgment are only one gate away, but instead of risking an immediate trial, they stand here to atone and crowd up our routes. Excuse me," he said, raising his voice, "archangel and soon-to-be archangel coming through. Move out of the way, please." The crowd moved slightly, but Lucifer figured it was probably more due to the giant wings or long tail they would get smacked with if they didn't move than Michael's polite but annoyed request.

Lucifer laughed. "Catholics aren't so bad," he said, twisting to pass around a group of souls. "Protestants and the like already arrive immediately at Judgment. Imagine the trial line if all the Catholics showed up there, too."

Michael shuddered, conceding the point. "Better than going straight to… the other place, I suppose," he said. The word *Hell* was not often spoken in Heaven. While Heaven was an idyllic form of Earth, splendid with life and light, Hell copied an aspect of the planet known for destroying life: fire. Irredeemable spirits were sent to the fiery pit for endless penance. It was a place of fear and pain and an unpleasant topic, to say the least.

"Only cursed souls spend eternity burning," Lucifer agreed.

Lucifer and Michael stepped around some rhubarb plants and paused. Standing in front of them were the giant, pearly gates themselves, shrouded so completely in mist that nothing could be seen beyond them. A solemn man in a dusty brown robe stepped out of the fog.

"Nice to see you again, Peter," Michael said, nodding.

Peter turned slowly towards Michael and Lucifer with a long-suffering look. He said nothing.

"Right," Lucifer muttered. "Nice to see us, too."

"Anyway," said Michael, glancing at Lucifer with a warning tone in his voice, "I have Lucifer here for a meeting with the Almighty."

Peter did not move. If anything, Lucifer thought the anguish in his eyes grew greater.

"Fine. We'll follow protocol," Michael said, tail swishing in irritation. "I, Archangel Michael, will safely escort Angel Lucifer to an audience with the Anointed One, the Friend of Sinners, the Prince of Peace...." As Michael listed all the names of God, Lucifer tried to remain calm. He knew some of the ways in which he helped people went against tradition, but help was help. Surely this meeting was about his promotion, not to reprimand him, as the last one had been. That meeting, about fifty thousand years ago, had not gone well. He had been summoned and told in no uncertain terms to follow the way of the Lord exactly or face the consequences. Lucifer had tried, he really had, but sometimes he needed to break the rules. He would whisper to a wife to lie to her husband (to avoid a beating) or encourage a young man to kiss a young woman, although she was married (to an older man she didn't love). By encouraging a lesser sin, he was avoiding a greater sin. Lucifer took a breath. He was being foolish; this meeting was surely about his promotion.

"You may enter," stated Peter, in a voice that Lucifer thought sounded like a rusty church bell, and Lucifer realized Michael must have finally run out of names. The gates swung open.

Lucifer clapped Peter on the shoulder as they passed into the mist. "Always a pleasure."

Inside the gates was a vast expanse of bright nothingness. It was a peaceful place but a place that was distinctly not of Earth. Michael and Lucifer exchanged a nod and half a smile. Then, Lucifer knelt, closed his eyes, and began to pray.

"Speak to me, Heavenly Father," he murmured, following the formal language required for such an event, though it felt strange on his tongue.

Instantly, a deep and powerful voice slammed into his head. *Lucifer, my child. You wish to be an archangel. You feel you have been overlooked.*

"Yes, Holy Father," Lucifer said.

I have not forgotten you, said the voice. Lucifer felt his heart leap. He was finally going to become an archangel and get his crown of light. *You are not worthy.*

For a second, Lucifer forgot how to breathe. "I—I am worthy!" he protested when he had regained control, although he felt like he was going to throw up. He leapt to his feet and looked around for the source of the voice, but of course saw only Michael and nothingness. Lucifer clenched his fists and continued speaking. "I answer prayers. I give people what they want. I make them happy."

You answer prayers in My name but go against My way. You give what is wanted but not what is needed. You control without consent. You confuse happiness with instant gratification.

"Both will make someone smile," countered Lucifer. He knew he shouldn't, knew it meant he would probably never be an archangel, but couldn't resist adding to his argument. "The people are hungry, and tired, and sick. They pray and pray for help, but you never answer. I do. I grant them food, love, health, whatever they want. I ease their pain."

Those who suffer in their Earthly life are given joy in their eternal life, said the voice of God. *By providing them meaningless comforts, you jeopardize their endless bliss. I have seen your actions, heard your thoughts; I know you condone stealing and killing and sin. This is not My way.*

"They steal only what their neighbors will not give," exclaimed Lucifer, eyes figuratively and literally blazing. "They kill for a cause—life, home, love—"

My children are murdering one another, said the voice. *I lost five civilizations today alone due to your influence, Lucifer. You aid those corrupted by evil, those that wish to harm instead of help, in their wicked desires. Not all prayers are meant to be answered. You have failed to follow My way.*

"Your way," muttered Lucifer. He ignored Michael's wide eyes and vigorous head-shaking. "Your way has people dying in agony. Your way causes suffering. My way is better. It provides relief, satisfaction—"

To go against My way is to go against Me. You use My name in vain, justifying sin in the name of happiness. You are not fit to be an angel.

Lucifer's head was spinning. He had anticipated no longer being eligible for archangel. To not be an angel at all... that was something he had never considered. It was a fate worse than death. He needed an escape.

"Mercy," he said, throat dry. "I ask for mercy."

I gave you mercy fifty thousand years ago, when I told you to re-dedicate yourself to My way. You have lost your right to mercy. You will be Lucifer, the light-bearer, no more. You will be Satan, the adversary, he who goes against My way, who promotes sin and encourages evil. I will not grant you a halo. Take instead these horns as a reminder of your wrongdoing.

Suddenly, a burning pain pierced the top of Satan's head. Physical transformations were not supposed to hurt, but this was something else: a brand. He dropped to the floor, gasping for breath. His sunglasses fell off and cracked. He was dimly aware of Michael shouting, asking if he was okay. Satan bared his teeth in the semblance of a smile. He did not feel okay. Finally, the pain died down. Satan reached one shaking hand up to the top of his head and hissed as he cut himself on the razor-sharp horn he felt there.

A metallic scent filled the air and the space darkened, as it does before a thunderstorm. Satan realized he was about to be zapped with a lightning bolt and blasted into oblivion. Though he had seen justice served this way before, Satan had never expected to be on the receiving end of a lightning strike. He didn't think he deserved infinite nothingness; he had served faithfully for millennia. He knew it was true, what the King of Heaven and Earth had said—he went against His way, and by extension, God himself. If Satan was honest with himself, he knew that sometimes the lines between right and wrong blurred, but he tried to do the right thing. He tried to help.

Apparently, Michael felt the same. "Wait!" he shouted to the air, taking a step forward. "I have given my vow of protection. I humbly suggest exile instead of oblivion, Heavenly Father."

The metallic taste in the air disappeared, and Satan sighed in relief. He could handle a few thousand years slumming it with the humans on Earth. Exile was not common in Heaven, but not entirely unheard of. If he did everything right, he could get reinstated as an angel in a millennium or two. Slowly, to steady himself, Satan stood.

Exile, said God. *A moral suggestion. Still, you must face the consequences of your actions. For your sin, you must leave My kingdom. I damn thee, Satan, to everlasting Hell. You, and those you turn against Me and My way, will burn forever and never know peace.*

Satan didn't remember Michael leading him out past the pearly gates and through Purgatory to a little hidden wall of rocks. He barely remembered Michael commanding the rocks to split and a portal to Hell to open. As he surveyed the swirling abyss of rocks and darkness, Satan was not aware of much except *you will burn forever and never know peace.* He reached up to touch his new horns again, careful not to hurt himself this time. The cut he'd gotten earlier from his horns would almost certainly scar. Worse, it had gotten blood on his nice suit.

As Satan listened to the rocks knock against one another as they twisted and turned within the portal, he briefly considered attempting to hide or flee, but quickly discarded the notion. He wouldn't ask Michael, archangel that he was, to choose his side. The King of Kings was omnipotent and omnipresent and omniscient; nothing got past him and nothing ever would. He was well named the Almighty.

"I guess this is the part where I leave for eternal damnation," Satan said, once again staring into the portal.

"I guess so," said Michael. Satan knew Michael didn't mean to say goodbye with such a lackluster statement; Michael was probably just unable to think of anything else to say. Besides, sentiments like *I'll see you later* or *take care of yourself out there* didn't really seem appropriate.

"I'll miss you," Michael said.

Satan glanced up briefly from the portal and nodded. He could feel the temptation to blame Michael for his current predicament; after all, he'd been the one to suggest exile in the first place. Somehow, Satan couldn't bring himself to hate his old friend. They had been through so much together, slain so many demons. Michael had only offered what he felt would be a lesser but still suitable punishment. He'd had no way of knowing God would exile him to Hell instead of Earth. Satan knew Michael was good almost all the way through and that any sliver of evil was due to his own influence. "It's been an honor to know you," said Satan. He didn't realize the words were true until he had spoken them.

"And also to know you," said Michael, attempting a smile despite the tears in his eyes.

"We'll meet again," Satan said, steel in his voice. "I can promise you that." Something was burning in his chest, something that cried out for justice against the wrongs he had just suffered. No, not justice—revenge. He would do what he had to do, become the King of Hell if he must, convert as many souls as he needed to destroy the Heavenly Father. He had until the end of time to do it.

"You're full of it," said Michael. Satan appreciated his friend's attempt to cheer him up and decided to play along.

"If by 'it,' you mean incomparable charm and a sparkling personality, then yes, I am full of it."

"Go to Hell."

Satan stared at him. The fire in his eye sockets brightened.

"Right," said Michael, clearing his throat. His tail flicked from side to side. "Sorry."

Satan snorted, shook his head, and prepared to step into the swirling rocks. Then he paused. Turning around, he gave Michael a brief but well-meaning hug, careful not to crush Michael's wings or snag his hair on Satan's new horns. Then, Satan took a deep breath, straightened his crooked tie, and stepped backwards into the portal to Hell.

AUTHOR'S NOTE

I've heard it said that if you don't have something to say you shouldn't write. For the most part, I agree with and abide by that. However, I think there is purpose in writing for fun and fun alone.

Literature does not have to be sad to be worth reading. It is a crime to ignore the beauty in life when it is around that which life is centered. Fiction allows the reader an escape from the modern world, a way of coping with the tragedies of quotidian life.

"It Started With Light" does not have a deeper meaning, unless the reader wishes to assign it one. It was created simply because I love to write. Re-imagining traditional stories is a concept that has always interested me, and rewriting Satan being exiled from Heaven in a more light-hearted tone was, well, fun.

LA CHANTEUSE ET LE CHANSON

La chanteuse d'opéra a ouvert les rideaux un peu. À l'extérieur, elle voyait les spectateurs. Ils lui attendaient chanter. Elle a fermé les rideaux et a respiré profondément. Bientôt, elle a dû aller sur scène.

La chanteuse d'opéra a eu un secret: elle n'aime pas chanter. Chaque fois qu'elle a commencé à chanter, elle ne pouvait rien entendre. Les gens disaient qu'elle avait une belle voix.

« C'est magnifique », ils disaient. « C'est le soleil et la lune et les étoiles. »

La chanteuse d'opéra n'était pas certaine.

Quand elle chantait, elle aimait imaginer le son. Certaines nuits, quand elle chantait en colère, elle était un lion. Elle imaginait qu'elle rugissait bruyamment, mais les spectateurs n'avaient jamais peur. Quand elle était triste, elle imaginait le son était la pluie. Elle ouvrait sa bouche et pensait de gouttes de pluie dans une rivière. Les spectateurs ne remarquaient jamais. Quand elle était heureuse, elle a chanté des oiseaux.

Une fois, quand la chanteuse d'opéra était une nouvelle, elle en avait eu marre. Elle n'avait pas chanté. Elle avait crié. Le théâtre avait été silencieux et sa gorge avait été douloureuse. Puis, à sa consternation, les spectateurs avaient commencé à applaudir. Ils l'avaient adorée.

Elle a regardé l'horloge. Il était presque le moment. Peut-être qu'elle serait une tempête ou un chat ce soir. Remarqueraient-ils? Soudainement, elle a eu une idée.

La chanteuse d'opéra a ouvert les rideaux complètement et a traversé à la scène. Les spectateurs la regardaient. Elle a fermé les yeux et a ouvert sa bouche pour chanter.

Elle n'a pas imaginé qu'elle était un animal ou un son. La chanteuse d'opéra n'a rien imaginé et elle était silencieuse.

Après un moment, elle a ouvert les yeux pour regarder les spectateurs. Au début, ils ne comprenaient pas. Puis, ils étaient en colère.

«Boo!» ils ont dit. «Où est la musique? Pourquoi tu ne chantes pas?»

Lentement, la chanteuse d'opéra a fermé la bouche. Les spectateurs ont commencé à jeter des tomates à la chanteuse d'opéra. Elle n'a rien dit. Puis, souriant largement, elle a quitté la scène.

AUTHOR'S NOTE

I'm sorry, did you think it would be in English?

I will not translate this piece from French to English as that would defeat the purpose of writing it. Instead, I will summarize. "La Chanteuse et le Chanson" describes an opera singer who has the most beautiful voice in all the world, but there is a catch: what she sings she cannot hear. She brings joy to others but never to herself. She hears only silence.

In order to make music, the singer thinks of something she wants to channel; a ferocious lion or a light rain or a flock of birds, for example. She creates music simply by imagining a sound and opening her mouth. She can easily and beautifully express the ideas and emotions of other creatures or things. Her own thoughts, however, remain silent.

The singer decides, just once, to take back control of her voice through silence, sharing with the audience what has been inside her head the entire time. The audience is confused for a moment, then begins to jeer. The singer walks off stage, reputation ruined but dignity intact. She never sings again.

I had originally titled this piece "Publication" because it reflects the irritation I was feeling with the business of writing at that time. In fact, I wrote this story to spite traditional ideas about publication; it's written in French, uses clichés, and is an awkward length. It's essentially unpublishable. Yet here it is.

In its final form, "La Chanteuse et le Chanson" is my love letter to anyone starting a writing career searching for that first publication, balancing originality and marketability. And so, to fellow beginning authors, I offer one simple and yet challenging piece of advice: you should like what you create.

•• [8] ••

ADRENALINE

It was not until I was sixteen years old that I realized I was not alive.

It was spring and nearing the end of my sophomore year. As I attempted to reflect on my memories of the past eight months, I found myself unable to recall anything extraordinary. I had no stories of hilarious mistakes because I was too careful to make them; I had no tales of late night adventures or road trips because I stayed in and studied and slept. In short, my youth was dissipating every day and I had nothing to prove I had ever lived.

From this realization came the desire to do something. It was like an itch I couldn't scratch; I wanted it so desperately, but I couldn't define what this something was. I had become a prisoner early on in my life to responsibility and caution. My dad died in a car crash when I was two; my mom was an overworked single parent. Money was as scarce as her time. So, I looked after myself more than most children. I craved the teenage insensibility I felt I had been deprived. I wanted to be young and heartless and a little bit stupid; I wanted the recklessness in life and love I had only ever watched from afar. Not once had I been given the simple teenage pleasure of making mistakes.

"Jenna! You will not believe the patriarchal nonsense I just dealt with," announced my friend Ro, jolting me out of my reprieve. I blinked, a little startled, as she sat down in the hideous red and orange plaid library chair across from mine. After school, the library became a center of socialization for people who were not cool enough for the cafeteria or who didn't have a strong enough nicotine addiction for the parking lot. "Mr. Pesit—from Algebra II—stops class, says, 'Aurora, your shorts do not meet our dress code standards,' and sends me to the principal's office. The principal's office! Can you believe that?"

I assured her that I could not. Ro was a tall, curvy girl with short platinum blonde hair and a nose ring. We contrasted one another well; I had long, dark hair I never knew how to style, neutral makeup, and a tendency to wear sweatshirts with combat boots. Ro wore almost exclusively bold lipstick and tight clothing. Today, for example, her lipstick was hot pink, which matched her deep V-neck shirt. The idea of anyone, particularly a high school math teacher, attempting to tell her what to do or wear was, indeed, unbelievable.

"So anyway, Principal Johnston let me off with a warning, because at least he is a decent human being, but now I'm on probation from *Little Shop*. Imagine if I had to quit the musical because of a stupid dress code violation," she said, utterly disgusted.

"I can't imagine it," I said, laughing. "How could the chorus line possibly function without you? I'm kidding, Ro, I'm kidding. We have rehearsal today, by the way. Also, when did you get back? You weren't in second period—"

"Jen," she interrupted, eyes sparkling, "Zachary Jones is right behind you."

"He is not," I said without looking. Zach and I had been childhood friends until we went to separate high schools and lost contact. I twisted around. Sure enough, there he was, wearing suspenders with jeans and rubbing the chain of his silver locket. It was the kind of necklace I assumed had been surgically grafted onto him at his birth and would not be removed until his death, if then. Once, in middle school, I had asked him who was in it. He'd refused to answer.

"I know you," said Zach, a grin spreading across his features, and I realized we had been making eye contact. "Jenna Robinson."

"Zachary Jones," I responded, smiling back. We got up and moved around the tables and chairs toward each other a little awkwardly. I wasn't sure if the confines of social convention dictated a hug or a handshake or something else entirely. Zach broke the standoff by opening his arms and I embraced him.

"Idiots," I heard Ro mutter.

"What are you doing here?" I asked him.

"Just transferred," he said. "I'm here until graduation."

We became very close very quickly. Since we lived near one another, it was established that I would drive him home from school. As the student director of *Little Shop of Horrors*, I had to stay after school every day for rehearsals, which meant Zach had to stay. There, Zach met Isabelle Irving, a casual friend of Ro's and an acquaintance of mine. Although Isabelle was the costume designer of the musical, with the ability to create all sorts of wacky styles, her own wardrobe consisted almost exclusively of converse and flowy shirts with flowers on them. She had a soft yet sassy character and, best of all, a van.

She'd gotten the van for her sixteenth birthday during the second week of musical rehearsals. We immediately named it Audrey III, after the man-eating Venus flytrap in *Little Shop,* Audrey II, which itself was named after the female lead (the original Audrey).

After the show on a beautiful May day, the four of us went for a drive in Audrey III. The AC didn't work and one of the doors didn't open, but the windows rolled down and it played music so loudly we couldn't hear ourselves screaming along, so we loved it. It was there, in that old beige van with the people who would become my world, that I began to feel truly alive. As the warm spring breeze caressed my face and the gorgeous melody sang to my soul, I felt all my senses awaken. I quickly

70

became addicted to the feeling; once experienced, it was impossible to forget.

We remained friends even after *Little Shop of Horrors* ended and the enthusiastic reviews of our show were all that were left to document its existence.

It was soon revealed that each of us was a little bit screwed up. Ro's secret I knew. In fact, the whole school knew. Her father had cheated on her mother, our school counselor, with his receptionist. Ro professed often how annoying it was to be a contemporary cliché, but underneath her bluster was real pain. She would get violently sick for weeks or months at a time, missing school. Interestingly, none of the doctors her mother took her to could find the cause of her mysterious illness. I couldn't tell if she was trying to cope or die. Zach's dad was a deadbeat drunk. Zach confessed to me once that he was terrified of ending up like his father. I tried to reassure him that not all children become their parents, but the tense look never quite left his eyes. Isabelle (or Belle, as we now called her) would talk about anything and everything except her family. Her father was a pastor who could not accept his atheist daughter; their arguments contributed to her intense fear of confrontation. The less she was home, the less they would argue, so she often suggested driving somewhere in the evenings. We were always glad to accept her offer.

Our place of holiness became the diner. We came once a week to discuss life, love, and lack thereof. The first time we went, we ordered an appetizer sampler for the table and began to chat.

"Have you guys heard of the Kinsey scale?" Belle asked, reaching for a mozzarella stick. We shook our heads. "It's this scale to rate how gay you are. One is totally straight, ten is totally gay. Most people fall in the middle. I'm probably like a three."

"Same," said Ro, bobbing her platinum head in agreement. "Maybe a four on the right day."

"Eight, easy," said Zach. None of us were surprised.

"What about you, Jen?" Belle asked.

"I don't know," I said, feeling heat rise in my face. The truth was, I did know and had suspected for a while, ever since middle school. In English, I sat next to a gorgeous girl who wore red-tinted chap stick and captured my thirteen-year-old heart within a week of meeting her. Now, at sixteen, I had a massive crush on a girl named Jessie. It had started when she was upset over something (I didn't remember what) and passionately ranting about it under the glaring neon lights of the fast food restaurant where we both worked. Soon, I was not listening to the content of her speech; I was distracted by the melodic way her voice rose and fell and the tears that shone in her eyes that she was too strong-willed to let fall. It was then that I realized I was absolutely entranced by her.

"Seven," I said, as quietly as I could.

"What?" Belle asked.

"Seven," I said louder, making eye contact with her.

"It's about time," Ro muttered, while Belle and Zach made *ooh* noises. I took a bite of spinach dip, blushing, and the conversation moved on.

Driving home, I touched a hand to my face. It was sore from laughing so much. I fantasized that I could sense little smile lines appearing on my skin. I wanted proof that I had something to smile about, proof that I was finally living.

Still, I had that unrelenting itch. Was I reckless enough? The four of us, in Audrey III, would drive up to the state penitentiary late at night. It was a little bit dangerous and more than a little bit stupid, but it was the highest point in our small city and we loved it. When we parked the van and looked out at the beautiful warm city lights, lazily watching the minuscule cars and tiny people go about their lives, we were content. In fact, it may have been the only time the itch fully subsided. We were scientists observing the human experience.

It was summer then and as temperatures rose, so did our passions. I wanted more.

Zach and I would find a house under construction, sneak in, and give ourselves a tour. It was exactly the sort of pointlessly dangerous activity I craved. One night, we found a house almost complete; the only unfinished section appeared to be the kitchen and back door. Since the door wasn't installed yet, we decided to go in that way.

Unfortunately, the construction crew hadn't finished restoring the lawn, and what should have been a back porch attachment overlooking a grassy plane was instead a hole in the back wall of the house above a giant, muddy crater. Zach, a head taller than me, was able to push himself up to the doorway and climb in with little problem. I, on the other hand, could not hoist myself up—a fact Zach found far too amusing.

"You look ridiculous," he said, laughing. "You're so—" Suddenly, the color drained from his face as he looked across the yard at the street to my left. "Jenna, get up," he said urgently. "There's a cop car coming down the street. They'll see you."

Time slowed down. I knew our house-hunting was probably otherwise characterized as breaking and entering and had considered the possibility that we would get caught. Now that it was a real threat, I realized I would do anything to avoid it. Heart pounding, I tried to lift myself up again. I pushed up six inches and collapsed; the crater was too deep and too slippery for me to crawl out of. I tried and failed again. I could hear the crunch of a car on gravel growing louder and louder.

"Zach, help me!" I whispered, surprised to find tears of panic in my eyes. "I can't get up!"

"They'll see me, too!" he hissed back, but after a moment's pause, he rushed over, grabbed my arm, and hauled me inside. We moved quickly to the other side of the room to avoid the police car's headlights as it passed. I didn't realize we were still clutching each other until he moved his hand from me to his locket.

"Who's in it?" I asked impulsively, gesturing to the necklace. We were both breathing hard.

After a moment's hesitation, Zach opened the locket, showing me the small, reflective oval. "No one," he said. His eyes looked black in the night. "That's the secret." Zach closed the locket with a soft click.

I didn't know what to think of that.

"Thanks, by the way," I said instead. My heart was still pounding in my ribs. "For going back for me."

"Don't expect me to do that again," he responded. "I could've pulled a muscle."

I nodded, but I was secretly grateful for the experience. Now that the terror was over, I loved the feeling of my heart pulsing against my ribcage. *Alive,* I thought. *I'm alive.*

My excursions with Ro were much less high-stakes. It is far easier to create an identity than redefine one. Since we had been friends before the group was formed, we knew one another well. It would have seemed almost out of character for us to do anything truly stupid. Instead, we talked.

"My mom lost her job," I told her, sitting in my car, eating ice cream we had bought at the gas station. "Apparently she got fired three weeks ago. I had no idea; she never told me. I only found out because my aunt talked about it at lunch Saturday. I guess I'll be working extra hours until she finds something."

"My dad wants me to have dinner with his girlfriend," Ro responded. She took a bite of her mint chocolate chip, careful not to smear her light blue lipstick. "His receptionist girlfriend is the same age as my sister. He says it'll be good if I meet her, help to make us a family. He already had a family."

"Our lives are jokes," I said, and though I heard myself laughing, I couldn't remember a time I had felt more hollow.

"Can't argue with that," she snorted. "Turn up the music, Jen. I don't want to be able to think for a while."

I did as she asked.

My time spent one-on-one with Belle was somewhere between the high-intensity of Zach and low-intensity of Ro. When she or I wanted to escape our houses, we would text each other. One of us would pick up the other and we'd listen to music and drive and drive until we made it out of the constraints of the city. We'd talk about life for a while and eventually turn around. Directionless, we would return to the very place we had fled.

I came to pick her up for one of those drives. As soon as she got into my car, Belle said, "Thanks for picking me up; I needed to get away from my dad. He keeps pressuring me to get confirmed, like that will somehow make me religious. I don't want to talk about it," she added, noticing my look. "Also, you're late."

"Sorry," I said. "Swear I have a good reason."

She looked at me suspiciously. "You're smiling. Is it about Jessie?" she asked.

I rolled my eyes. "Not everything in my life is about Jessie," I said. "She's still dating Stephanie, I'm still single, and she still doesn't have any idea I was madly in love with her."

"Was?"

I shrugged. "Did you know she asked if I was free tonight?"

"No," Belle said. "Is that why you were late? You can go hang out with her, if you want. I'll be fine. Depressed and alone, but fine."

"I *don't* want to. That's the thing. I've been waiting forever for the chance to spend some time with Jessie outside of work, and when she finally asks me to hang out, she wants me to meet her in the East side park, but only for an hour, because then the mom of the kids she's babysitting will show up." I blew a strand of hair out of my face. "I just . . . don't feel anything anymore. I don't know why."

"She didn't deserve you, anyway," Belle reaffirmed. I snorted.

"That flattery makes me glad I was late. Look what I brought," I sang, reaching into the backseat of my car and pulling out a cardboard drink tray with Earl Grey tea and coffee. Taking a sip of the tea, I passed the coffee to Belle. "Turtle latte, extra caramel, right?"

She stared at me.

"Tell me that's your order," I said. "This is going to be really embarrassing if that's not your order."

"It is," Belle said. We locked eyes.

"Just so you know, I'd rather be here with you than out with Jessie," I told her. Belle smiled back at me, a tentative smile that grew slowly but happily.

It occurred to me that in another life, I might fall for Belle. However, my newfound inability to feel anything about anything was adequate at preventing that. Since finding out about my mother's unemployment, it was like my emotions were on a switch set to off. I became more and more reckless. I was a junkie of my own making; I needed to feel something and I didn't care what.

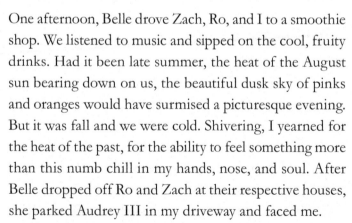

One afternoon, Belle drove Zach, Ro, and I to a smoothie shop. We listened to music and sipped on the cool, fruity drinks. Had it been late summer, the heat of the August sun bearing down on us, the beautiful dusk sky of pinks and oranges would have surmised a picturesque evening. But it was fall and we were cold. Shivering, I yearned for the heat of the past, for the ability to feel something more than this numb chill in my hands, nose, and soul. After Belle dropped off Ro and Zach at their respective houses, she parked Audrey III in my driveway and faced me.

"Jen, there's something I need to tell you," she said.

I gestured for her to go on. She squeezed her eyes shut, as though she was in pain. "I have a crush on you," she blurted.

"Oh," I said. It was easy to see how someone could love her; Belle was gorgeous. She was caring and soft and smelled like jasmine conditioner. Still, I felt the same nothing towards her that I felt towards everything, with the exception of a vague sense of discomfort that I couldn't return her feelings. I realized I had let the pause continue for too long.

"Forget it," she snapped, pink coloring her cheeks. She unlocked my door. "I'll see you in school."

I stared at her a moment longer. It was like my brain had split into two parts; the Jennas of past and present. Past Jenna was screaming at present Jenna to say something, anything, to ease the awkwardness and repair the fractured friendship. Past Jenna was disgusted with present Jenna as I nodded, opened the door, and left. I didn't look back.

Winter began to creep into our souls. Though we were in the musical together once again, this time performing *And Then There Were None*, Belle and I tended to skirt around one another. It was uncomfortable to talk to her and uncomfortable not to. Ro and I remained close. She approached me after rehearsal one afternoon.

"Zach's been telling people you're gay," she stated, eyes flashing.

My blood turned to ice as genuine fear coursed through my veins. "Why?" I asked.

"I don't know," she answered. "Talk to him."

I waited until we pulled into his driveway. We were silent much of the ride, both of us preoccupied with the embarrassing comedy of errors that had been tonight's performance. I looked at Zach, snowy sunlight shining down on his face. Blue shirt, white skinny jeans, black coat. And of course, his necklace. It occurred to me I wanted to take his stupid, empty locket and choke him with it.

"You told everyone in the musical I'm gay," I said, fighting to keep my voice level.

"Oh . . . yeah," he laughed. "Don't worry; I told them I'm gay, too."

My knuckles were white on the steering wheel. "That wasn't your decision to make."

He looked sideways at me and frowned, as though finally realizing I was upset. "Jen, c'mon. They would've found out eventually."

"On my terms," I said, turning to make eye contact, steel in my voice. "They would have found out on my terms, in the way I want, when I want. Maybe I would have said bi instead of gay. Maybe I would have told only a few people instead of the whole musical. I guess we'll never know."

"They would have found out," he repeated. "You need to move on."

I stared at him, and it was as though I'd never seen him before. He didn't care about me; had he ever? He needed a ride and I had a car. He craved the adrenaline hunt just as much as I did; maybe it had never been about friendship. Slowly, as I stared into his eyes, I felt my heart turn to dust and begin to crumble.

"Get out, Zach," I said quietly, closing my eyes and leaning my head against the seat.

He stayed put. "Jenna . . . " he started, and lightly touched my arm.

"Get out of my car!" I shouted, snatching my arm away, suddenly furious. Tears sprung to my eyes.

Zach looked at me, and I imagined I could see him come to a realization. Watching the mascara stream down my cheeks, it seemed he was finally starting to understand the consequences of his actions. He rushed out of my car, looking back at me as though making a last-ditch attempt to see if I was okay. I wasn't.

The drive home was only a few blocks but I debated crashing the entire way. I wished desperately for the nothingness I'd been swimming in the last few months. Now, I was drowning in a sea of heartache. Wiping my eyes, I grabbed my phone and called Ro. Her mother answered and told me she wasn't feeling well. She wouldn't be in school for a while. Thanking her, I hung up. I wasn't sure if I was crying for my mother's unemployment or Belle's distance or Zach's betrayal or Ro's unreliability or some combination of everything. I pulled into my garage, parked my car, and sobbed. It was winter and everything was dead.

A song came on the radio and I paused, hiccuping

slightly. It was the very first song we had listened to together, back in May. I turned it up, the bass shaking my car, and thought of how I had felt in Belle's beige van: awake. Had I not, over the last almost-year, accomplished what I'd set out to do? I'd made mistakes; some were humorous, some were not. The proof of my teenage escapades would live forever in my memories. I could still taste the melancholic remnants of what it was to be young and reckless and a little bit stupid.

I took a deep, shuddering breath and smiled, wiping away my tears. I was alive.

AUTHOR'S NOTE

"Adrenaline" is a coming-of-age story about an American girl determining who she is and who she wants to become.

The violently exalted youth culture in the United States—the feeling that youth is the prime of life and yet ever-fading, the pressure to succeed young or not at all—weighs on Jenna's conscience as she tries to make the most of her remaining teenage years. She searches desperately for some kind of meaning in life which has otherwise eluded her.

My favorite thing about Jenna is her voice. Everything to her feels immediate and important and incredible, but at the same time, she struggles with finances, sexuality, and friendships. And yet despite the mature concepts that Jenna must learn to manage, her voice is distinctly that of a teenager: dramatic, headstrong, and a little bit angry.

ACKNOWLEDGEMENTS

To Oliva McGovern, my wonderful and brilliant editor; to Caleb Venkatrathnam, for his unwavering support; and to everyone else who made this dream a reality.

AFTERWARD

Writing a book, as a general idea, has been on my bucket list for years. The concept of *The Drawing Board* specifically came into being after I rediscovered some short stories I'd written over the last two years saved on my laptop. Due to COVID-19, I was spending a lot of time indoors, so I decided to do something productive with that time: I would combine my seven favorite previously-written pieces with a brand new one and publish them together in a short story collection.

The Drawing Board got its name from the idiom "back to the drawing board," meaning to restart. I really liked the idea of restarting or rebirth in the context of a short story collection; each individual story acts as a restart, with new characters, settings, and plots. The cover of this book is a blank piece of paper on a drawing board: it's a physical representation of a new beginning. Plus, I thought the idea of this collection as a base and being able to literally return to *The Drawing Board* later on in my career was humorous and even a bit clever. I hope you enjoyed reading *The Drawing Board* as much as I enjoyed writing it.

Made in the USA
Monee, IL
22 December 2020